by BERNARD WABER

Lovable Lyle

Houghton Mifflin Company, Boston, 1969

for Gary

Everyone loved Lyle the Crocodile.
The Primm family, with whom he lived,
loved him dearly, of course.

And the bakery lady loved him.
She always gave Lyle a cookie;
his favorite kind, with colorful
sprinkles on top.

And Mr. Delight, the ice cream man, loved him.
He always invited Lyle to climb aboard
his truck and clang the bell.

And Bird loved him.
"Love Lyle! Love Lyle!"
squawked Bird.

And the children loved him. They always called for Lyle to come out and play.

And in return, Lyle loved the whole, wide, wonderful world.
He didn't have one single enemy in it . . .
or so he thought.

One day, quite mysteriously, a note addressed
to Lyle was slipped under the door of the
house on East 88th Street.
"Dear Lyle," Mr. Primm read to him. "I hate you.
I hate you more than anything. I hate you so much
I can't stand it."
And the note was signed, "Your enemy."
Everyone was so surprised.
"Oh, how dreadful!" cried Mrs. Primm. "Whatever
reason could anyone have for hating Lyle?"

"Don't worry about it, Lyle," said Mr. Primm. "Just keep being your wonderful self, and try to forget this ever happened."

Lyle went off to bed that night trying hard to forget. Still, as he switched off the lights and gazed down upon the empty street below, he could not help sadly thinking, "Somebody out there hates me."

The next day, Lyle lost himself
in play, and managed to forget all
about the note . . .

only to be reminded by a second one
delivered as mysteriously as the first.
"Dear Lyle," read Mrs. Primm,
"I hate you even more today than I did
yesterday—if that is at all possible."
And again, the note was signed, "Your enemy."
"Oh, these horrible notes have just got
to stop!" Mrs. Primm cried out desperately.

Lyle wanted the notes stopped too. He was
so unhappy about them. There were days he just
couldn't be coaxed out of the house.
He began to wonder if he was growing ugly.

He practiced smiling.

At other times, he was outdoors being his
friendliest to everyone, hoping somewhere, somehow,
his "enemy" would see what a nice crocodile
he really was.
He smiled big, big smiles. And he waved big,
big waves, greeting one and all as warmly and as
joyously as he knew how.

He performed all of his sure-fire tricks
to amuse people . . .

and practiced new ones
at home each night.

13

He was kind, helpful, and courteous.
He held doors open for people loaded down
with heavy packages.

He offered his seat
on crowded buses.

He shared his umbrella.

"My, doesn't he have nice manners!"
one lady remarked.
"I've never seen anything like it,"
answered another.

Poor Lyle worked so hard
at being nice, he was positively
exhausted by the end of the day.

Indeed, all of the Primms were unhappy about the notes. Each time they heard someone approaching outside, Joshua or Mr. Primm, sometimes the entire family would rush for the door, in hopes of catching the note writer in the act.
They even took turns watching from the window.

One afternoon, Mrs. Primm, Joshua, and Lyle
came across the words, ''Down with crocodiles,''
brazenly scrawled upon a fence near home.
Mrs. Primm tried hopelessly to erase the
nasty words with a tissue.

"Well, Lyle," she said, as they made their way home, "it seems no matter how much we may think we want to, it isn't always possible to please everyone, or be liked by everyone."

As they approached their house, they noticed the small figure of Clover Sue Hipple, the new girl in Joshua's class.

By the time they reached the door, Clover was gone.
But resting under the door was still another note.
"I just don't know if I can bring myself to read it,"
sighed Mrs. Primm. But she forced herself just the same.
"Dear Lyle," she read, "I wish you would go away and
never come back—ever, ever, ever again."
Once more, it was signed, "Your enemy."
Sadly, Mrs. Primm crumpled the note in her hand.

Oddly, during the next several days,
Mrs. Primm and Lyle found themselves running
into Clover Sue Hipple almost everywhere
they went. At the supermarket, they discovered
her peeking out from behind a huge
display of cornflakes.

Another time, they
caught a glimpse of her,
hiding behind a tree.

And again, one afternoon,
they discovered her crouched
behind a mailbox.

Each time, Mrs. Primm smiled
and tried to say hello.
And each time, Clover skittered
off before she had a chance.

One day, as she was about to leave the house,
Mrs. Primm glanced down just in time to see another
note wiggling its way into the house.

Quickly, she opened the door.
Before her, wide-eyed with surprise,
and still clutching the note,
stood Clover Sue Hipple.

"Clover dear, please don't run away," cried Mrs. Primm,
"I would like to speak with you . . . about Lyle. Has
Lyle done something to make you angry with him?"
"He takes my friends away from me," Clover burst out.
"He what?"
"He takes my friends away from me," the little girl
said again. "When Lyle comes out, my friends run away. They
run to play with him. And they play with him all of the
time. I never have fun when Lyle is around."
"But why can't you play with Lyle too?" asked Mrs. Primm.
"Because," answered Clover.
"Because of what?"
"Because I'm not allowed. My mother said I'm not allowed
to play with crocodiles."

"Why don't you invite Clover's mother here to meet Lyle?" suggested Mr. Primm that night. "I'm sure when she sees for herself how gentle Lyle really is, she won't mind if Clover plays with him."

Mrs. Primm telephoned Clover's mother the very next day.
"Lyle and I want so much to meet you," she said. "Could you join us for tea tomorrow afternoon?"
"I would be delighted," answered Mrs. Hipple. Mrs. Hipple made a note of the address and all was cheerfully arranged.

"Now, who is this nice Mrs. Primm?" Clover's mother wondered. Setting up the new house had left her little time for meeting neighbors.

"And who is Lyle?" The only Lyle she knew of, was that wretched Lyle the Crocodile creature, who lived with a most peculiar family somewhere nearby.

"Imagine!" she clucked disapprovingly, "a crocodile living among decent, respectable people."

But this Lyle? "He must be that nice Mrs. Primm's husband," she decided. "Of course."

"Remember now, Lyle," said Mrs. Primm, the
following afternoon, "when Mrs. Hipple arrives,
greet her with your very best manners.
Offer to take her coat. And when you have
hung it neatly in the closet, join us
in the living room. Understand?"
Lyle nodded.
"Good," said Mrs. Primm, humming as she
returned to the kitchen.

When Mrs. Hipple arrived, Lyle started
down the stairs to meet her.
But then he stopped.
"Suppose she won't like me," the thought popped into his head.
Suddenly a wave of shyness came over Lyle. Suddenly, the last
thing in the world he wanted to do was meet Mrs. Hipple.
"Lyle! Lyle!" called Mrs. Primm.

"Lyle! Lyle! Where are you? We have company," Mrs. Primm
called again as she led her guest into the living room.
He wanted to go to her, but instead, and although he
kept telling himself it was absolutely the silliest, most
ridiculous thing he could possibly do, Lyle squeezed
himself into the hall closet and hid.

Mrs. Primm looked for him upstairs,
and she looked for him downstairs.
"I just can't imagine what has become of
Lyle!" he heard her exclaim.

Amid the tinkling of teacups, Lyle could hear the voices
of the two women. They talked about this, that, and
everything under the sun. It was so stuffy and uncomfortable
in the closet, he began to wish they would talk about
Mrs. Hipple leaving.

At long last Lyle heard Mrs. Hipple say,
"I must be going now," and Mrs. Primm say,
"I'm so glad you came, and so sorry you missed Lyle,
but I do hope you will be meeting him real, real soon."
Then Lyle heard the handle of the closet door turn
as Mrs. Primm said, "Here, let me get your coat."

The instant the door opened
Lyle fell out upon both women.
Mrs. Primm let out a sharp gasp.
And Mrs. Hipple definitely screamed.

"Are you all right? Are you all right?" Mrs. Primm
cried out, as they struggled to their feet.
"Take him away! Take that monster away from me!"
Mrs. Hipple began to shriek.
"Oh, please, he won't hurt you. I promise he won't hurt you,"
Mrs. Primm tried to reassure her. "Look at him! He's more
frightened than you."
"LET ME OUT OF HERE!" Mrs. Hipple shrieked on.
"LET ME OUT OF THIS TERRIBLE HOUSE!!"

Mrs. Primm opened the door as Mrs. Hipple,
her hair and clothes all in a rumple
stumbled from the house.
"If that crocodile ever so much as crosses
my path, I'll have him arrested," she
called back over her shoulder.
"This is supposed to be a
nice neighborhood, you know."

"Poor Lyle," sighed Mrs. Primm, that night,
"now he's afraid he's going to be arrested.
We're just going to have to think of something
to take his mind off his troubles."

On the first warm day, the Primms
knew just what to do for Lyle.
"We'll take him to the beach,"
they decided.

"Swimming has always been Lyle's
favorite sport," smiled Mrs. Primm.
"And he's by far the best swimmer
in the family," her husband added.

While Mr. and Mrs. Primm made themselves comfortable, and Joshua started on a sand castle, Lyle took a running dive into the water.

Lyle's water stunts delighted everyone close by . . .

. . . everyone, that is, except Mrs. Hipple who
had just arrived, and with Clover was
dunking her feet.
Mrs. Hipple set out at once to find a lifeguard.

"Lifeguard! Lifeguard!" she cried,
"do you permit crocodiles to bathe here?"
"Certainly not," answered the lifeguard.
"Well, it might interest you to know, there
is a crocodile bathing out there, this very minute."
Mrs. Hipple pointed to the spot, where
she had seen the crocodile.

Suddenly, everyone on the beach was
looking and pointing; but not at a crocodile.
They were pointing to a little girl,
thrashing about helplessly, in the water.
"Clover! Clover!" cried Mrs. Hipple.
"She's drowning!"

The lifeguards immediately pushed off to the rescue.
But Lyle raced to the scene before them.
"There's a crocodile out there!" someone gasped.
"No, its Lyle," called Mrs. Primm, standing nearby.
"I mean, it's Lyle the Crocodile."

Lyle brought a very wet, but happy Clover
safely back to shore.
"Hurrah for Lyle!" the crowd shouted.
"Oh, Lyle, dear friend," sobbed Mrs. Hipple,
"how can I ever thank you enough?"

Everyone was so proud of Lyle.
He was immediately appointed honorary lifeguard.
He was then given a hat, a sweatshirt, and
a silver whistle.
"Lyle, you are a hero," said the head lifeguard.
"Feel free to come here and save people from drowning
anytime you choose."

The next day, a note addressed to Lyle, was found
under the door of the house on East 88th Street.
"Oh, no, not again!" Mrs. Primm moaned.
"Dear Lyle," read Mr. Primm. "I love you."
I love you more than anything. I love you so much
I can't stand it."
And the note was signed:
"Your friend for life, Clover Sue Hipple."
"P.S." Mr. Primm continued. "May I play with you today?
PPS. My mother said it's all right."

Lyle smiled . . .
one of his big, big smiles.